ONCE UPON A CHRISTMAS TIME...

A Feast of Seasonal Stories & Poems

HUTCHINSON
LONDON SYDNEY AUCKLAND JOHANNESBURG

First published in 1999

3 5 7 9 10 8 6 4 2

This edition © Hutchinson Children's Books 1999
Text and illustrations © individual authors and
illustrators; see Acknowledgements

The authors and illustrators have asserted their right under
the Copyright, Designs and Patents Act, 1988, to be identified
as the authors and illustrators of this work

First published in the United Kingdom in 1999 by
Hutchinson Children's Books
Random House UK Limited
20 Vauxhall Bridge Road, London SW1V 2SA

Random House Australia (Pty) Limited
20 Alfred Street, Milsons Point, Sydney
New South Wales 2061, Australia

Random House New Zealand Limited
18 Poland Road, Glenfield
Auckland 10, New Zealand

Random House South Africa (Pty) Limited
Endulini, 5A Jubilee Road, Parktown 2193, South Africa

Random House UK Limited Reg. No. 954009

A CIP catalogue record for this book is available from the British Library

ISBN: 0 09 176773 3

Printed in Singapore

CONTENTS

Shirley Hughes
WILD WEATHER

Winter is coming! The wind that blows
   Hard from the north, from the land of snows,
Nips the fingers and reddens the nose
And strips the tree.

The track is sticky with mud and mire,
And crows string like crotchets along the wire,
And wanderers think of home and fire,
And so do we.

Maggie Russell

THE THREE BEARS' CHRISTMAS PARTY

Illustrated by Anthony Lewis

IT WAS CHRISTMAS TIME and the three bears who lived in the house on the edge of the wood decided to give a party.

They each wrote invitations to their friends. The Great Huge Bear wrote great huge invitations; the Middle-sized Bear wrote middle-sized invitations and the Little Wee Bear wrote little wee invitations (mostly to rabbits).

Then they cleaned the house from top to bottom and decorated it with holly and mistletoe.

"We need a Christmas tree," said Great Huge Bear. "Tomorrow I'll go out into the wood and dig one up."

Middle-sized Bear who was longing to have a day on her own in the kitchen to do all the cooking said, "Little Wee Bear can go with you. I'll give you both a packet of sandwiches."

In the morning, after Great Huge Bear and Little Wee Bear set off, Middle-sized Bear got her cooking pots and her scales and butter and flour from the cupboard and she made Bath buns and rock buns and soft batch buns and whole wheat buns and some great huge Derby scones and some little wee doughnuts. And she enjoyed herself very much.

Meanwhile Great Huge Bear and Little Wee Bear had gone deep into the wood and had found the perfect tree. First they sat down and ate their sandwiches and then Great Huge Bear took his spade and began to dig in a circle round the roots of the tree.

All at once the spade hit a large stone; it flew up in the air and Great Huge Bear fell on to his back with his leg bent underneath him. Little Wee Bear was very alarmed. He tried to help Great Huge Bear to his feet for his knee was badly twisted.

It took them a long time to get home. Middle-sized Bear was looking for them anxiously.

She made Great Huge Bear soak his leg in hot water. Then she bandaged it up and said he must go to bed.

"What about the party?" wailed Little Wee Bear. "And we haven't got a Christmas tree."

Middle-sized Bear thought of all the buns she had cooked. "We shall still have the party," she said. "Great Huge Bear may be better in the morning."

But in the morning Great Huge Bear had a sore head as well as a bad leg. However, he said grumpily that he would come downstairs and sit by the fire.

The guests came promptly at three o'clock. There were black bears, brown bears and grizzly bears, the bears from the post office and the bears from across the stream.

They all arrived together and they all tried to knock on the door at the same time.

There were no rabbits; they were afraid of getting trodden on.

The party was a great success. Everyone made a fuss of Great Huge Bear, who judged the winners of musical bears, musical statues, pass the honey pot and the treasure hunt.

Then they each pulled a cracker and sat down for tea.

As the last bun disappeared and the bears lay back feeling extremely full, there came the sound of squeaky voices singing, "Good King Wenceslas looked out . . ."

Little Wee Bear flung open the door and a gang of rabbits giggled nervously. Beyond them stood a Christmas tree.

The rabbits, with help from a squirrel or two, had felt sorry for Little Wee Bear and had decorated a tree in the wood.

All the bears crowded outside – and Great Huge Bear found he could walk after all!

It was a perfect end to the party.

Gino Alberti

SIMON AND THE SNOW

Illustrated by Sieglinde Wolfsgruber

SIMON LIVED IN A LITTLE HOUSE high up in the mountains. It was winter and he was happy, for of all the seasons he loved winter the best.

He loved the snowflakes and the icicles; he loved to take long rides on his sledge, and most of all he loved to build jolly round snowmen with carrot noses.

One day Simon looked around him and noticed grass growing and new buds on the trees. Spring had come early.

Simon was sad: he wished it could be winter for ever.

But that night, as Simon lay sleeping, the air turned cold again. Softly, it began to snow.

The garden was covered in white and the windows were speckled with frost.

As soon as Simon woke up, he noticed that something was different.

He ran to the window and looked out in wonder at the snow. The winter had come back again! It was as if his wish had come true.

"The snow is back! The snow is back!" he cried out joyfully. He put on his woolly hat and mittens and ran outside. He began to build a whole family of snowmen. His mother gave him some carrots for the noses and some straw for the arms. Simon was very happy.

The next day was even colder. As soon as he was up, Simon went to play with his snow family. But what had happened? He ran from one snowman to the next. The twig arms and the carrot noses were gone! Who could have done such a thing?

There was no time to think for Simon's mother was calling him in to breakfast. Later, as Simon fetched some new noses and arms from the kitchen, he made a plan.

That night the sky was so clear you could count the stars. While his mother slept, Simon, wrapped up warmly, collected his cat Mutz and climbed out through the window. Together they trudged through the snow until they came to a very tall tree. "Here's a good place," said Simon as he climbed up. Mutz followed. They were cold and frightened, but even if they had to stay up all night they would catch the carrot thieves.

For a long, long while everything was still. Then, suddenly, Simon saw something move. Gathering up his courage he climbed down the tree and hid behind a snowman. He could hardly believe his eyes – all kinds of animals were coming out of the forest and they were greedily eating everything they could from the snowmen.

Simon could see that the poor animals were very thin and hungry. The return of the winter had buried their food under deep snow. He quietly took a couple of steps towards them, but the animals ran away in fright.

Later that morning, Simon told his mother what had happened. "The poor animals are starving," she said, and she gave him a basket of hay to take to them.

Simon carried the basket to the edge of the forest. The animals gazed at him hungrily. "Don't be frightened," Simon whispered.

Very, very slowly a little deer dared to come forward. Then, when the other animals saw it was safe, they too came out of the forest. There were fawns and rabbits and stags and birds. Simon fed as many as he could, but there wasn't enough food for everyone. Then Simon had an idea.

He put the basket on his back and set off to the village. Shyly, the animals followed him. The village people stopped what they were doing to watch the strange little procession making its way down the mountain.

Everyone wanted to hear Simon's story. He told them about his snowmen and how he had discovered the hungry animals. The whole village wanted to help. At the entrance to the village the grown-ups built a big feeding trough. Then all the children ran home to fetch food for the animals.

Every day, the children brought new supplies. There was enough for all.

Soon the snow melted and the days began to grow warmer. The smell of new grass was in the air again. Spring had come at last - this time to stay. The animals could go back to the forest for good.

From that time on, Simon still loved the winter, but now he loved the spring as well, for he knew the importance of the seasons.

Susie Jenkin-Pearce

PENGUIN

PEPPI WAS A PENGUIN and he lived at the zoo. He hated his concrete enclosure. He hated the way people leaned over the rails and stared at him. He hated quarrelling for food at mealtimes.

One morning, Peppi looked around him. A penguin's life is not a happy one, he thought, and he stretched his wings and sighed.

That afternoon a careless little boy dropped something into Peppi's enclosure.

Down,

down,

down

it fell.

It had an orange beak and a black coat and plippy ploppy feet, just like a penguin. But it wasn't quite the same.

"My name is Poppy and I'm a toy," it said. "And one that is not loved, for my owner has wandered off and forgotten me already."

"I'll be your friend, and I'll love you," said Peppi. And from that moment, the two were inseparable.

One day Poppy told Peppi about Father Christmas, who had given her to the little boy. "He lives at the North Pole," she said. "There are reindeer and polar bears. The sea is frosty cold and the whole land is covered in ice and snow. I'd love to see Father Christmas again. Perhaps then he would give me to someone who really loved me."

When Peppi thought of the land of ice and snow, his feathers began to tingle. Suddenly, he knew that was where he belonged.

"Let's fly to the North Pole!" he cried. "If you want to see Father Christmas again, you shall."

It was a dangerous but exciting plan.

All morning Peppi did exercises to strengthen his wings.

Peppi borrowed some
extra feathers from a seagull
and Poppy tied them to his
wings. When he was ready, he
climbed to the top of the
penguin slide and launched
himself off. Whoops!
It was no use. He
had forgotten that
penguins can't fly.

They decided to hide in the keeper's fish bucket.

"When it is taken back to the sea," said Poppy, "we can jump out and stow away on a ship."

So after the next feeding time, the two friends hid in the keeper's empty bucket. Soon they were rattling along in the back of a big lorry. The journey lasted a day and a night. When the lorry finally stopped, the driver was astonished to see two small penguins leap out and run away.

"Which ship for the North Pole?" cried Poppy.
"Over there," replied a passing seagull.

Poppy and Peppi were soon aboard and on their way across the ocean.

After three stormy days and nights at sea, Poppy noticed that the air was turning colder. Peppi looked through a porthole - there were lumps of ice floating on the sea.

"We're here!" he cried.

Poppy climbed on to Peppi's back and clung on tightly while he bravely leaped from the porthole. Nothing could stop them now.

The two friends swam ashore.

"I'll have to go," said Poppy, tearfully, and her little beak quivered. "I must catch Father Christmas before he sets off on Christmas Eve."

"Goodbye, and good luck," said Peppi, sadly. "I'll miss you."

Peppi wandered off. He loved the feeling of the smooth cold snow in his toes and the cool fresh air under his wings.

Very soon he met some polar bears. "Good afternoon, friends," he said, politely. "Can you tell me where the penguins live?"

"Penguins! Penguins!" cried the polar bears in their loud deep voices. "What are penguins?"

"I'm a penguin," said Peppi, proudly.

The bears looked him up and down. "We've never seen anything like *you* before," they said.

Peppi began to cry. "But I know that penguins live in the land of ice and snow," he moaned.

The polar bears just laughed at him and wandered off into the white mist.

Now Peppi felt very lost and alone. Hours passed, but Peppi could see nothing but the great white waste that stretched on for ever.

All of a sudden, he thought he could hear a sound; a lovely jingly sound like little bells.

And there, through the mist, came Father Christmas on his sleigh. And best of all, Poppy was sitting beside him, waving. Father Christmas gently lifted Peppi aboard his sleigh.

"You are right – penguins do come from the land of ice and snow," he said. "But they live at the *South* Pole, not the *North* Pole! I'll take you there."

Father Christmas drove his reindeer across the wintry sky, over the sea and far away. As they flew over the zoo, Peppi could see all his friends in the enclosure. "They will never know the frosty sea and feel the cold, arctic wind under their wings," he said, sadly. "If *only* they could come too."

"And so they shall," replied Father Christmas. For on Christmas Eve he can make wishes come true.

Father Christmas flew his sleigh into the enclosure and every penguin, from the biggest to the smallest, climbed aboard. And off into the sky and across the world they flew to the South Pole.

All the penguins of the South Pole had gathered to welcome them, as if they knew they were coming.

"Here is your real home," said Father Christmas.

He gave each penguin a special present. "And this is your real home too," he said to Poppy, "for I think you *have* found someone who really loves you."

34

And he was gone.

John Richardson

BAD MOOD BEAR AND THE BIG PRESENT

CHRISTMAS WAS COMING and Bear was writing a letter.

Dear Father Christmas
Please please please can I have a red racing car.
I have been a good bear all year.
Thank you very much.
Bear xxx

Bear put the letter in an envelope, stamped it, and addressed it to Father Christmas in the North Pole.

Bear posted the letter on the way to school.

"It's for Father Christmas," Bear told Mum.

"Oh," said Mum. "What have you asked him to bring you?"

"It has to be a secret," whispered Bear. "Or it won't happen."

At school, Mr Baboon was busy organising the Nativity play.

He read out from a list. "Goat and the Pig twins can be the three kings," he said. "Fox can be a shepherd and Bear can be one of his sheep."

"Can't I be a king too?" growled Bear, waving his paw furiously.

"Sorry, Bear," said Mr Baboon. "There are only three kings in the story."

Bear felt a bad mood coming on.

For the rest of the week Goat and the Pig twins teased Bear.

"Baa baa Bear sheep," they chanted. "Have you any wool? Ha ha!"

"I don't care," growled Bear. "Anyway, Father Christmas is bringing me a red racing car, so there!"

Bear stopped still and put his paw over his mouth. Now they'd made him tell his secret and it wouldn't come true!

The play was on the last day of school. It wasn't much fun being a sheep and Bear was fed up and miserable when it was time to go home. To cheer him up, Mum took him to see Father Christmas at the local toyshop.

Bear spotted a beautiful red racing car in the shop window.

"Look, Mum, look!" he shouted, jumping up and down.

Inside the shop, Bear wandered over to a crowd gathered around a robot.

Mum called him several times, but he pretended not to hear.

"Come here this instant, you bad bear!" she snapped.

"Oh, all right then," said Bear rudely. "Keep your hair on."

"Ho, ho, ho," laughed Father Christmas kindly. "What a cross little bear."

Oh no! thought Bear. Father Christmas thinks I'm naughty and he won't bring me a red racing car.

Soon it was Christmas Eve. Grandad and Grandma were decorating the Christmas tree. Bear could see some chocolate snowmen near the top. When nobody was looking he climbed on a stool and tried to grab one. But he wibbled and wobbled and fell on the tree, bringing it all crashing down.

"Do try to behave," said Dad, picking him up and drying his eyes. "Father Christmas is watching you. Now off to bed. I'll be up in a minute to read you a story."

"I hate Christmas," sobbed Bear as he marched up the stairs. "Father Christmas won't bring me my racing car, now that I've been naughty."

On Christmas morning Bear woke up to find a stocking hanging from the end of his bed. Inside were a tangerine, a pencil, some nuts, a rubber and a blue balloon that was very hard to blow up.

But Bear wanted his big present.

He rushed downstairs to find the Christmas tree surrounded by parcels and packages. Without even saying good morning, he grabbed the biggest one and started opening it.

"Now hold on just a minute," said Grandma. "Just you wait until everyone is here."

Bear felt his bad mood coming back.

It seemed like ages before everyone had come downstairs and it was time to open the presents.

"Me first!" bellowed Bear.

Mum gave Bear a stern look and handed the first package to Grandad. Next she gave one to Grandma and everyone waited until she'd opened it. Then Dad gave one to Mum and Mum gave one to Dad.

Bear thought he would burst with impatience.

"Ooh, thank you," he cried as Mum handed him his present.

It was square and it was very big.

Bear tore off the wrapping paper. Inside was . . . a big beautiful cuddly toy tiger. Bear's mouth dropped open.

"But . . . " he said. Then before he could stop himself, he had thrown the beautiful toy tiger across the room.

"Now, now, Bear!" said Mum.

Bear burst into tears. "But I wanted a . . . oh, never mind," he whined. "It's all because I haven't been good."

"Oh, cheer up, Bear," said Mum. "He's a lovely tiger."

"Nobody understands," wailed Bear and he stormed upstairs to his room.

A few minutes later Dad came upstairs and gave Bear a big hug. He told him everyone was missing him. Bear didn't want to miss Christmas so he swallowed his pride and went downstairs with Dad.

As Bear walked in everyone cheered. His Uncle Bob and Aunty

Lil had arrived with Cousin Charlie. Everyone was wearing funny party hats.

Bear felt a big smile creep across his face, and as he smiled a warm Christmassy feeling spread through his whole body.

Suddenly Bear was laughing and joining in all the fun.

"Happy Christmas, everyone!" he cheered.

"Happy Christmas, Cousin Bear," said Charlie, handing him a big present. Bear opened it. Inside was . . .

. . . a shiny red racing car!

"My wish has come true," gasped Bear. "It's just what I wanted!"

"Me too," said Cousin Charlie rather sadly.

"Well, we can share it then!" said Bear. And as the two little bears played together Bear felt the same warm Christmassy feeling spread over him again.

After a wonderful Christmas lunch, they played games. Bear thought it was the happiest Christmas ever.

"Thank you for my racing car," he said to Cousin Charlie. Then he looked up.

"And thank *you,* Father Christmas," he added, hugging his lovely new toy tiger close to his heart.

Peter Bowman

TINY TED'S
WINTER

"IT'S SNOWING," said Mouse . . .
"which must mean that Christmas is coming."

"I'd better write my letter to Santa Claus."

"Robin, will you please take this to Santa?"

"I'll write a letter too. Now, what would I like?"

"Oh no, I've missed Robin. Never mind, I'll take it to Santa myself."

"Wheeee!"

"Oops!"

"That was lucky."

"Sorry, I can't stop. I'm looking for Santa Claus."

"Perhaps this is where he lives."

"I'll ask inside."

"Hello, I'm looking for Santa
Claus."

"You just missed him," said a
big bear.

"Oh dear, oh dear. It's getting
dark . . . I'd better hurry."

"Where *is* he? I've looked *everywhere*."

"One last place to try."

"Ah ha! No presents. That means he hasn't been here yet . . ."

"I'll wait for him to come
down the chimney . . ."

"Mmm, that was tasty."

"I think I'll have a little nap."

"Hey! What's happening?"

"Oh no, don't put me in the rubbish."

"Phew! Where am I?"

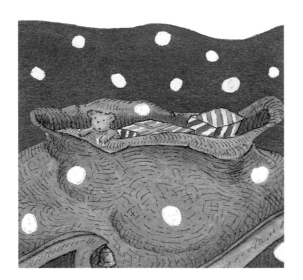

"Oh dear, I've lost my letter. I won't get a present now."

"Hey, put me down!"

"Where am I *now?*"

"Christmas won't be the same without Tiny Ted," said Mouse. "Now, what did Santa bring me . . . ?"

" . . . TINY TED!"

"I've got a present too," said Tiny Ted. "Santa must have got my letter after all!"

Jane Hissey
JOLLY SNOW

IT WAS COLD AND GREY OUTSIDE. Jolly Tall, the giraffe, had been gazing out of the window for days.

"What are you waiting for?" asked Rabbit.

"I'm waiting for it to snow," said Jolly. "It is winter, isn't it?"

"It doesn't *always* snow in winter," said Rabbit.

"In fact it hardly ever does," said Duck gloomily.

"I know where there's some snow," said Little Bear. "It must be left over from last winter. I'll get it for you."

Without waiting to explain, Little Bear rushed out of the room.

In a moment he was back again, carrying a large glass bubble. Inside the bubble they could see a little house and a tree covered in a layer of tiny white snowflakes.

"Is that all snow does?" asked Jolly, staring into the bubble. "Does it just lie around making things whiter than usual?"

"Of course not," said Little Bear. "That wouldn't be any fun. You can make it into balls and throw it."

"Or slide on it," said Zebra, as she joined the others.

"And jump into heaps of it," said Rabbit, "and make footprints."

"You can build things with it too," said Duck.

"Goodness," said Jolly. "There doesn't look enough of it for that."

Holding the glass bubble tightly, Little Bear jumped up and down. A flurry of snowflakes leaped from the tiny house and tree and rushed around inside the glass. "Look at it now!" he squeaked.

"There's still not enough to make a snowball," said Jolly.

"And anyway you can't get it out," said Duck.

"Wait a minute," said Zebra, "I know where there's lots of snow."

She led the way to the kitchen, where Bramwell Brown was busy making some special biscuits. To stop the biscuit dough sticking to the rolling pin, he was shaking flour from a flour shaker.

"Whoopee!" cried Zebra, dashing under the falling flour. "I'm in a snowstorm."

In no time at all, her black stripes had almost disappeared.

Rabbit tried to gather up a pawful of the flour. "It's not very good for snowballs," he said. "It doesn't stick together."

"But it's perfect for DOUGHBALLS," cried Little Bear, rolling up a piece of dough and throwing it at Rabbit. The doughball stuck to Rabbit's bottom and looked like an extra tail.

"This flour-snow doesn't come off," said Zebra, jumping up and down trying to shake herself clean.

"I think you are going to need a bath," said Bramwell.

He filled a dish with soapy water and the snowy Zebra climbed in. She began to splash about, sending bubbles flying everywhere. "It's still not coming off," she grumbled. "It just gets stickier and stickier."

"Flour and water make a sort of glue," said Duck. "You'll probably have to stay white for ever."

"No you won't," said Bramwell kindly. "We'll get you clean."

All the scrubbing and splashing made even more bubbles.

"Snow-bubbles!" cried Little Bear, jumping about, popping them with his paws. "Hurry up, Zebra, we want to use your bath as a snow-machine."

After lots of rubbing and scrubbing, Zebra's stripes at last reappeared. The others wrapped her in a warm towel and looked into the bath.

"What have you done with all the bubbles?" asked Little Bear.

"Bubbles never last," said Duck, "and anyway they would have made very sloppy snow. Why don't we go and see if Old Bear has any ideas?"

Old Bear was in the dining room cutting out paper decorations. He'd made paper stars, paper bells and paper lanterns. He'd even made paper snowflakes.

"You can't really play with these," said Little Bear, trying to slide on a snowflake.

"No, you can't," said Old Bear, rescuing his decoration. "They're only meant for looking at."

"We want some snow for Jolly," said Rabbit. "Snow you *can* play with."

"What about these?" said Old Bear, scattering a blizzard of paper pieces in the air.

"Lovely," said Rabbit.

"And nice and slippery too," said Little Bear, taking a run at a heap of them and skidding along on his bottom.

"What we need is a sledge," said Rabbit, "or Little Bear will wear out his trousers." He fetched a cardboard box and Bramwell cut away the sides. Duck tied a string to the front and they pulled it along to test it.

"Now if we had a slope," said Rabbit, "we could whizz down it in the sledge."

"I don't think I could," said Jolly. "I wouldn't fit in it."

"Never mind," said Bramwell. "You can help with the slope." Bramwell Brown disappeared into the bedroom and came back pulling a large white sheet. He gave a corner to Jolly. "Now," said Bramwell, "when the others climb on, lift up your end and they should slide all the way down."

Rabbit and Little Bear pushed the sledge onto the sheet and climbed in.

"There's only room for two," said Rabbit.

"Don't worry," said Zebra, "I'll slide on my tummy."

As soon as they were ready, Little Bear called out to Jolly: "One, two, three, GO!"

Jolly and Bramwell lifted their end of the sheet.

Nothing happened.

"Wobble it a bit," called Rabbit. "We seem to be stuck."

Jolly and Bramwell shook the sheet as hard as they could and suddenly the toys found themselves sliding very fast to the other end.

"Look out," cried Little Bear, as the sledge whizzed off the sheet, across the room and crashed into the wall on the other side.

"I think we need a softer landing," said Rabbit, fluffing up his flattened fur and helping Little Bear to his feet. He piled up a heap of cushions against the wall and then all three toys bravely climbed back onto the sheet.

"Ready, steady, go!" they called to Jolly.

Up went the sheet. Down went the toys – straight into the heap of cushions. As they landed clouds of feathers puffed out of a little hole in one of the cushions and filled the room.

"Look - it's feather-snow," cried Little Bear, making the hole bigger with his paw and jumping on the cushion to make more feathers escape.

Very soon all the toys were jumping in the feathers. They rolled in them, crawled through them and piled them in heaps.

"Is this like snow?" asked Jolly.

"It's better," said Little Bear. "It doesn't melt and it doesn't make you cold."

"Let's put some round the windows," suggested Rabbit, "then it will look as if real snow has settled there."

He climbed up to the windowsill and began to pile feathers in each corner. When he reached the third window pane he stopped and looked, then looked again.

"Somebody has already done this one," he called to the others.

The window did have a white covering around the edges . . . but it was on the *outside*.

"It isn't feathers," cried Little Bear excitedly. "It's real snow!"

All the toys crowded onto the sill and stared out of the window in amazement.

"Now we can play outside," said Zebra.

"Well, actually - it looks a bit deep for me," said Little Bear.

"And a bit cold for me," said Old Bear.

At that moment, Bramwell Brown came into the room carrying a huge plateful of his special snowflake biscuits.

"I think what you need is some of *my* snow," he said.

Jolly Tall thought about the flour-snow and the feather-snow, the bubble-snow and the paper-snow. Then he looked at the real snow floating down outside.

"I really like all kinds of snow," he announced. "But," he added, munching a snowflake biscuit, "Bramwell's snow is probably the snow I like best!"

John Bush
IF MOOSES WERE GOOSES
Illustrated by Peter Weevers

"O dear! O dear! O deary me!
How I wish a moose could ski!
The trouble when it snows and snows is
We get stuck up to our noses.

"And O the effort to get out!
The time it takes to move about!
You just can't find a thing to chew.
O *what* is a poor moose to do!

"I wish, O how I wish we mooses
Could fly above the ground like gooses,
Because at times like this the truth is,
Wings and feathers have their uses."

Pat Hutchins

THE SILVER CHRISTMAS TREE

SQUIRREL WAS BUSY decorating his tree for Christmas. He hung garlands of holly and ivy around the branches, bunches of bright red berries between the branches, and pine cones on the tips of the branches. And although it looked nice, it didn't look quite nice enough.

So he hung strings of polished nuts on the tree, tied bunches of mistletoe around the tree, and stuck dried heads of wheat into the pine cones on the tips of the branches. And although the tree looked nicer, it still didn't look nice enough.

Squirrel worked so hard, and so late, that it became too dark to see the tree at all.

But at that very moment, right on the very top branch of the tree, a beautiful silver star appeared. The tree looked wonderful! Squirrel was delighted. He would show his lovely silver Christmas tree to his friends on Christmas Eve, as a special present.

Squirrel slept happily that night and didn't wake up until the sun was quite high in the sky. Then he raced down the tree to admire his silver star. But when he gazed up into the branches, the lovely star had vanished! And his beautiful silver tree wasn't silver any more.

Squirrel searched in the tree, around the tree, and under the tree. But he couldn't find the silver star. So he went to ask his friend Duck if he'd seen it.

His friend Duck was hiding a parcel in the rushes. Ah, thought Squirrel, my friend Duck has found my star for me. "Duck," he said, "is that my star you've found hidden in the rushes?"

Duck smiled. "Aha!" he said. "You will have to wait until Christmas Eve to find out what is hidden in those rushes!"

So, thought Squirrel sadly as he walked away, Duck has my star.

On his way home he passed his friend Mouse, who was putting a parcel behind a stone wall. Ah! thought Squirrel. I knew my good friend Duck wouldn't take my star. I see Mouse has found it for me!

"Mouse," he said, "is that my star you've found hidden behind that stone wall?"

"Aha!" Mouse smiled. "You must wait until Christmas Eve to find out what is hidden behind that stone wall!"

So, thought Squirrel sadly as he walked away, Mouse has my star.

Then he passed his friend Fox, who was tucking a parcel into his lair. Ah! thought Squirrel. I knew my good friend Mouse wouldn't take my star. I see Fox has found it for me!

"Fox," he said, "is that my star you've tucked into your lair?"

"Aha!" Fox smiled. "You must wait until Christmas Eve to find out what is hidden in my lair!"

So, thought Squirrel sadly as he walked away, Fox has my star.

But then Squirrel saw his friend Rabbit, who was slipping a parcel down his burrow. Ah! thought Squirrel. I knew my good friend Fox wouldn't take my star. I see Rabbit has found it for me.

"Rabbit," he said, "is that my star you're slipping down your burrow?"

"Aha!" Rabbit smiled. "You will have to wait till Christmas Eve to find out what is hidden in my burrow!"

So Squirrel went home and waited.

The next day Rabbit, Fox, Mouse and Duck arrived. "Happy Christmas, Squirrel!" shouted Rabbit, handing Squirrel a parcel.

This must be the star, thought Squirrel, but it felt too soft to be a star.

And it wasn't. It was a soft fluffy blanket.

"Thank you, Rabbit," said Squirrel sadly. "It will keep me nice and warm through the winter. It's the nicest blanket I've ever had."

"Happy Christmas, Squirrel," said Fox, handing Squirrel a parcel.

Fox must have had the star after all, thought Squirrel, but it felt too long to be a star.

And it wasn't. It was a long silky duster.

"Thank you, Fox," said Squirrel sadly. "It will do nicely for dusting my tree. It's the nicest duster I've ever had."

"Happy Christmas, Squirrel," said Mouse, handing Squirrel a parcel. So, thought Squirrel, it was little Mouse who had the star. But it felt too round to be a star.

And it wasn't. It was a little round corn cake.

"Thank you, Mouse," said Squirrel sadly. "It's my favourite kind of cake and the nicest cake I've ever had."

And then Duck handed Squirrel a parcel. Ah! thought Squirrel happily. This must be the star. But it felt too square to be a star.

And it wasn't the star either. It was a square basket, woven from rushes.

"Thank you, Duck," said Squirrel sadly. "It will be very handy for storing my nuts. And it's the nicest basket I've ever seen."

Then Squirrel pointed to his tree. "And there's my present to you," he said. But it was nearly dark, and his friends couldn't see anything.

But then all the animals stared in wonder, for soft flakes of snow were falling from the sky, and as they fell, the clouds parted. Climbing up to the top branch of the tree was the silver star, bigger, brighter, and more beautiful than ever.

The glow from the tree lit up Squirrel's face. "Happy Christmas, everyone," he whispered. "Happy Christmas!"

And all his friends thought it was the nicest present of all.

Max Velthuijs

FROG IN WINTER

WHEN FROG GOT up one morning, he realised at once that something was wrong with the world. Something had changed.

He went to the window and was astonished to see that everything was completely white.

He rushed outside in confusion. There was snow everywhere. It was slippery under his feet. Suddenly he felt himself falling over backwards . . . down the bank, into the river. But the river was frozen and Frog lay on his back on the cold, hard ice.

If there's no water, I won't be able to wash, he thought, shocked.

Shivering with cold he sat on the bank. Then Duck came hurrying towards him on her skates. "Hello, Frog," she said. "Nice weather today! Are you coming skating?"

"No, I'm freezing," replied Frog.

"But skating is good for you," said Duck. "I'll teach you."

So Duck gave Frog her skates and her scarf. She pushed him and he slid quickly across the ice, but not for long. Soon, he fell.

"Aren't you enjoying yourself?" said Duck. But Frog was nearly frozen solid and his teeth were chattering.

"You've got a warm feathery coat, but I'm just a bare frog," he said.

"You're right," said Duck. "You'd better keep my scarf, as I must be on my way."

Then Pig appeared with a basket of firewood on his back.
"Aren't you freezing, Pig?" asked Frog.

"Freezing?" said Pig. "No, I'm enjoying the fresh, healthy air.
Winter is the most beautiful season."

"You have a nice layer of fat to keep you warm. But what do
I have?"

Poor Frog, thought Pig. I wish I could help him.

One, two! One, two! Hare ran up. He was jogging in the snow.
"Hurrah!" he called joyously. "Sport makes you healthy! Hurrah
for sport! Three cheers for sport!

"Why don't you join in, Frog? It's great fun keeping fit."
"I'm freezing," said Frog. "You've got warm fur, but I have
nothing." Sadly, he went home.
The next day his friends invited him to have a snowball fight. But
Frog couldn't share in the fun.
"I'm freezing," he murmured. "I'm only a bare frog," and miserably
he stumbled home.

He sat next to the fire for the rest of the day, dreaming of spring and summer. He burned every last piece of wood.

When the fire went out he went outside to gather more logs, but he couldn't find any wood in the snow.

He walked and walked until he lost his way. Everything was white. Exhausted he lay down in the snow. A bare frog.

And there his friends found him.

"I'm freezing," whispered Frog.

"Come on," said Hare, and carefully they carried him home and put him to bed.

Hare collected wood and lit a fire. Pig cooked a nourishing soup and Duck cheered Frog up.

In the evenings, everyone listened while Hare read wonderful stories about spring and summer. Meanwhile, Pig knitted Frog a warm pullover in two colours. Frog enjoyed the attention from his friends. Winter is wonderful when you can spend it in bed!

Then the day came when Frog was well enough to get up. Without fur, fat or feathers, but dressed in his new pullover, he took his first steps in the snow.

"Well?" asked Hare curiously.

"It's good," answered Frog bravely.

So the long winter passed. But one morning when Frog opened his eyes he noticed at once that something was different. Bright light streamed in the window. Quickly, he jumped out of bed and ran outside.

The world was bright green and the sun shone in the sky.

"Hurray!" he cried. "It's good to be a frog. How wonderful. I can feel the sun's rays on my bare back."

His friends were happy to see Frog so cheerful.

"What would we do without Frog?" laughed Hare.

"I can't think," said Pig.

"No," agreed Duck, "life just wouldn't be the same without him."

Russell Hoban

THE MOLE FAMILY'S CHRISTMAS

Illustrated by Lillian Hoban

HARLEY MOLE and his son Delver did straight mole work. They tunnelled and they dug and they brought home the groceries. Harley and Delver wore overalls and thick boots and heavy work gloves. They wore thick glasses, because the whole Mole family was very nearsighted, and they had little lanterns in their caps, because they tunnelled in the dark.

They tunnelled in the springtime and the summer. They tunnelled through the autumn and through the winter, while Harley's wife Emma cooked and cleaned and washed the overalls. All three of them worked every single day, and all days were the same for them.

In the evenings Emma mended overalls and work gloves while Harley and Delver cleaned the lanterns and scraped the mud from their boots and rubbed them down with tallow.

When Delver's chores were done he polished up and sorted his collection of good-shaped stones and marbles and bits of

coloured glass that he had found while tunnelling. And sometimes he just sat around and thought. "Delver is a brooder," Emma used to say to Harley.

"Delver is a thinker," Harley always answered. "There's no telling what that boy might do when he puts his mind to something."

The Mole family's home was under the lawn of a house that had been empty for a long time. But that autumn a family of people moved in. And that winter, very early one morning when everyone was asleep, Delver tunnelled up through the earth and snow to have a look around.

At the back door of the house he found a house mouse looking at a calendar the milkman had left with Season's Greetings from the dairy. "Christmas is coming," said the mouse, and ran into his hole.

Delver thought about it all day, and at dinner he asked his mother and his father, "What is Christmas?"

"I have no idea," said Harley. "No idea whatever."

"Neither do I," said Emma. "Perhaps it's a people thing."

Delver thought about it some more, and that evening when his chores were done he went up to the people house. There he found the mouse again, dining on birdseed that had fallen from a feeder.

"What is Christmas?" Delver asked him.

"Several different flavours of paper and cardboard," said the mouse. "Fresh paste sometimes, and no end of ribbon, string, and nesting materials. Constant footsteps overhead, and no rest for anyone until he's come and gone."

"Until who's come and gone?" said Delver.

"Fat man in a red suit," said the mouse. "White beard. First there's a lot of stomping and snorting and jingling up on the roof. Then he comes puffing and wheezing down the chimney, puts knicknacks and candy in stockings, leaves all kinds of packages around, says 'Ho ho ho', and goes huffing and puffing up the chimney again. It's quite an odd thing, really, but he does it only once a year, and nobody seems to mind."

"What's in the packages?" said Delver.

"Skates and trains, dolls and whatnot," said the mouse. "The people children write letters, and if they've been good the fat man brings them what they ask for."

"Does he bring you anything?" asked Delver.

"No," said the mouse. "But then it's not my chimney, and I don't write letters. It's late," he said, "and I've got to be getting home before Ephraim Owl comes by on his evening rounds. Lovely night, isn't it? Look at all those stars!"

"Where?" said Delver.

"Up in the sky," said the mouse. "Where else?" He shook his head and ran back into the house.

Delver looked up, but he was too nearsighted to see the stars. When he squinted hard he could just barely make out a blurry brightness here and there, but that was all. He was still squinting up at the sky when a lady mouse came to nibble at the birdseed.

"The stars are especially fine tonight, aren't they?" she said.

"They certainly are," said Delver.

"Indeed," said the lady mouse, "it's almost like singing, you might say, the way they glimmer and shine, isn't it?"

"Yes," said Delver, "I think it is," and he went on squinting while the lady mouse went on nibbling. After a while Delver said, "Do you have any particular way of looking at the stars?"

"I just look up," said the lady mouse. "Of course I have seen people looking at them with telescopes, which is, I suppose, a particular way of looking. Look out!" she cried, and dived into the shrubbery, pulling Delver with her as old Ephraim Owl swooped down upon them.

"Hoo hoo!" said Ephraim as he flew up with nothing in his talons. "If not this time, then some other time," and he flew away, hooting and chuckling.

"You'd better keep your eyes open," said the lady mouse to Delver. "He almost caught you."

"I was thinking," said Delver. "What's a telescope?"

"I believe that a telescope is something like an extra, very far-sighted eye," said the lady mouse, "which would undoubtedly be helpful to anyone who might be somewhat nearsighted."

"Undoubtedly," said Delver. "Thank you very much. Good night." And he tunnelled slowly home, thinking about the stars.

All the next day as Delver worked with his father he thought about the stars he could not see, and after a while he began to cry.

"What's the matter?" said Harley, and Delver told him about the stars.

"I went above ground a time or two when I was young," said Harley. "I heard about stars too, and I know how you feel."

"There are telescopes," said Delver, and he told his father what the lady mouse had told him. "I wish I had a telescope," said Delver.

"So do I," said Harley. "It would be nice to see a few stars, just for the experience of it, you know."

"Maybe if we had a chimney," said Delver, and he told Harley about the fat man in the red suit.

"Ah," said Harley, "but that's a people thing. I never heard of a red-suited fat man giving anything to animals."

"And anyhow, we haven't got a chimney," said Delver.

"We've got a stovepipe," said Harley, "same as any other animals."

"You've got to have a chimney," said Delver.

"A people-sized chimney?" asked Harley.

"Well," said Delver, "it would have to be big enough for his hand with the telescope, at least."

"All right," said Harley, taking a deep breath and drawing himself up to his full height, "we'll make a chimney."

When Emma was told about the project she had many doubts. "I'd like to see the stars as much as anyone else," she said, "but we mustn't raise our hopes too high." Nevertheless she threw herself whole-heartedly into the work.

The Mole family made many night-time trips above ground for sand and cement for their mortar. Harley and Emma and Delver carried pieces of broken brick and heavy stones, always watching and

listening for the owl. Old Ephraim failed to catch them night after night, but vowed that he would sooner or later dine upon them. "The longer it takes," he said, "the better you'll taste." But the Moles kept working on their chimney in spite of Ephraim, and every night it grew higher.

The mouse who had told Delver about Christmas showed him how to spell out the words for his letter, and by the time the chimney was half built he was ready to mail it. The question was where to?

"I know he comes down," said the mouse, "so he must come from *up*. If I were you I'd send the letter up."

So the Moles found a very long stick and stuck it straight up in the snow, with the letter in a cleft at the end of it. The letter said:

To the fat man in the red soot -
All of us Mols down here hav bin good. We need a telaskop so we
can look at the stars. Maybe you dont giv things to aminals. Well
then I will swop my ston marbel and glass colleckshun for it. If that
is not enuf my father and I could work out the diffrens in tunels or
plane digging if you need enny tunels or plane digging dun.

Your friend,
Delver Mol

That night the Moles stopped work before Old Ephraim made his rounds, and so they were in bed when he passed overhead on silent wings. Old Ephraim saw the letter on the stick, snatched it up in his talons, stuck it in his back pocket, and flew away with it.

When the Moles came out the next night and saw that the letter was gone they were all very pleased.

"Well," said Delver, "now that it's been picked up, it's just a matter of time till the telescope comes."

Then the Moles worked very hard every night to finish their chimney. All of them hoped very much that the fat man in the red suit would come, but each of them thought that perhaps he might not come.

So just to make sure that Delver and Harley would have something for Christmas, Emma knitted new mufflers for them. Harley made a pair of pretty slippers for Emma and a pair of moccasins for Delver. Delver made a sewing box for his mother and a reading lamp with a green ginger-ale-bottle glass shade for his father.

Then all the Moles wrapped up their presents and hid them.

"Even if the fat man doesn't bring the telescope," said Emma to Harley and Delver, "he may leave some other little presents, you know."

"Just what I was thinking," said Harley.

"So was I," said Delver, and all three of them smiled to themselves.

When the Moles finished the chimney by the light of the moon on Christmas Eve they were all exhausted. They sat on top of their chimney and sighed happily, smiling up at the stars they could not see, and they were so tired that they all fell asleep sitting there in a row.

They were still sitting there asleep when Old Ephraim flew over. "Hoo hoo!" said Ephraim. "There they are just like a three-course dinner, all ready and waiting for me. I'll just swoop down, and they'll jump up and run – but they won't be fast enough."

Ephraim swooped down, but the tired Moles stayed fast asleep. "This doesn't seem quite right," said Ephraim, and he flew up again. "I'll hoot very loudly and count to ten to give them a head start and then I'll catch them.

"Hooo!" he hooted. "Wake up!" But the Moles would not wake up.

"Silly things!" said Ephraim. "They write letters about telescopes and stars and they sleep out in the open by the light of the moon. They certainly *deserve* to be eaten!"

Just then the midnight bells rang out in all the churches in the town, and the sound floated on the still air over the sparkling snow. Then from high up under the silent-singing stars there came a faint jingling of sleigh bells, and all at once Old Ephraim felt very jolly and full of fun.

"Wouldn't those Moles feel very foolish if they woke up and found themselves not eaten!" he chuckled. "And maybe just for fun I'll give that letter to whoever it is way up there in a sleigh. Maybe *he* knows the fat man in the red suit."

So it was that on Christmas morning the Moles woke up feeling very foolish for having fallen asleep out in the open, and found themselves not eaten. And there beside them on the chimney was a beautiful, shining telescope.

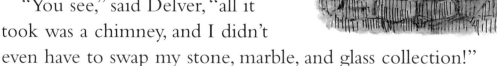

"You see," said Delver, "all it took was a chimney, and I didn't even have to swap my stone, marble, and glass collection!"

But the joke wasn't only on the Moles, because when Old Ephraim woke up that afternoon, he found a nicely wrapped package inside the door of the hollow tree where he lived. Inside the package was an elegant striped necktie, and a card that said:

Season's Greetings to a jolly good fellow
from the fat man in the red suit.

Best regards,
S. Claus

So that was the Mole family's first Christmas, and they were very pleased with it. On top of the chimney they made an owlproof observatory out of an upside-down flower pot, and then they were able to look at the stars in perfect comfort.

"I think Delver did very well to find out about Christmas as he did," said Emma.

"Yes," said Harley, "you never can tell what will happen when a boy like Delver puts his mind to something. Here am I, who never expected to see a single star, looking at all of them. I call that impressive."

"It really *is* like singing, the way they glimmer and shine," said Delver.

Even Delver's mouse friends, who were not at all nearsighted, found that they enjoyed viewing the stars through a telescope, and now they visit the Moles' observatory often.

Old Ephraim wears his necktie constantly, and although he still hunts the Moles regularly he has not yet managed to catch them.

There has been talk of using the Mole chimney next Christmas for all of the local animals, and the mice are already at work on their letters to the fat man in the red suit. So is Old Ephraim, who - being somewhat more knowledgeable - will address his letter to S. Claus.

Alf Prøysen

MRS PEPPERPOT'S CHRISTMAS

Illustrated by Björn Berg

THERE WAS ONCE a little old woman who went to bed at night like everyone else, but sometimes in the morning she would wake up and find that she had *shrunk* to the size of a pepperpot. As it happens her name was Mrs Pepperpot.

This was one of those mornings, and Mrs Pepperpot climbed to the top of the bed-post and swung her legs while she wondered what to do.

"What a nuisance!" she said. "Just when I wanted to go to the Christmas Market with Mr Pepperpot!"

She wanted to buy a sheaf of corn for the birds' Christmas dinner, and she wanted to get them a little bird-house where she could feed them every day. The other thing she wanted was a wreath of mistletoe to hang over the door, so that she could wish Mr Pepperpot a "Happy Christmas" with a kiss. But Mr Pepperpot thought this was a silly idea.

"Quite unnecessary!" he said.

But Mrs Pepperpot was very clever at getting her own way; so even though she was now no bigger than a mouse, she soon worked out a plan. She heard her husband put his knapsack down on the floor in the kitchen and - quick as a flash - she slid down the bed-post, scuttled over the doorstep and climbed into one of the knapsack pockets. Can you see her?

Mr Pepperpot put the knapsack on his back and set off through the snow on his kick-sledge, while Mrs Pepperpot peeped out from the pocket.

"Look at all those nice cottages!" she said to herself. "I bet every one of them has a sheaf of corn and a little house for the birds. *And* they'll have mistletoe over the door as well, no doubt. But you wait till I get home; I'll show them!"

At the market there were crowds of people, both big and small; everyone was doing their Christmas shopping, and there was plenty to choose from! At one stall stood a farmer selling beautiful golden sheaves of corn. As her husband walked past the stall Mrs Pepperpot climbed out of the knapsack pocket and disappeared inside the biggest sheaf of all.

"Hello, Mr Pepperpot," said the farmer, "how about some corn for the birds this Christmas?"

"Too dear!" answered Mr Pepperpot gruffly.

"Oh no, it's not!" squeaked the little voice of Mrs Pepperpot. "If you don't buy this sheaf of corn I'll tell everyone you're married to the woman who *shrinks*!"

Now Mr Pepperpot hated people to know about his wife turning small, so when he saw her waving to him from the biggest sheaf he said to the farmer, "I've changed my mind; I'll have that one, please!"

But the farmer told him he would have to wait in the queue.

Only a little girl saw Mrs Pepperpot slip out of the corn and dash into a bird-house on Mr Andersen's stall. He was a carpenter and made all his bird-houses look just like real little houses with doors and windows for the birds to fly in and out. Of course Mrs Pepperpot chose the prettiest house; it even had curtains in the windows and from behind these she watched her husband buy the very best sheaf of corn and stuff it in his knapsack.

He thought his wife was safe inside and was just about to get on his kick-sledge and head for home, when he heard a little voice calling him from the next stall.

"Hello, husband!" squeaked Mrs Pepperpot. "Haven't you forgotten something? You were going to buy me a bird-house!"

Mr Pepperpot hurried over to the stall. He pointed to the house with the curtains and said: "I want to buy that one, please!"

Mr Andersen was busy with his customers. "You'll have to take your turn," he said.

So once more poor Mr Pepperpot had to stand patiently in a queue. He hoped that no one else would buy the house with his wife inside.

But she *wasn't* inside; she had run out of the back door, and now she was on her way to the next stall.

Here there was a pretty young lady selling holly and mistletoe. Mrs Pepperpot had to climb up the post to reach the nicest wreath, and there she stayed hidden.

Soon Mr Pepperpot came by, carrying both the sheaf of corn and the little bird-house. The young lady gave him a dazzling smile and said: "Oh, Mr Pepperpot, wouldn't you like to buy a wreath of mistletoe for your wife?"

"No thanks," said Mr Pepperpot, "I'm in a hurry."

"*Swing high! Swing low! I'm in the mistletoe!*" sang Mrs Pepperpot from her lofty perch.

When Mr Pepperpot caught sight of her his mouth fell open: "Oh dear!" he groaned. "This is too bad!"

With a shaking hand he paid the young lady the right money and lifted the wreath down himself, taking care that Mrs Pepperpot didn't slip out of his fingers. *This* time there would be no escape; he would take his wife straight home, whether she liked it or not.

But just as he was leaving, the young lady said: "Oh, sir, you're our one hundredth customer, so you get a free balloon!" and she handed him a red balloon.

101

Before anyone could say "Jack Robinson" Mrs Pepperpot had grabbed the string and, while Mr Pepperpot was struggling with his purse, gloves and parcels, his tiny wife was soaring up into the sky.

Up she went over the market-place, and soon she was fluttering over the trees of the forest, followed by a crowd of crows and magpies and small birds of every sort.

"Here I come!" she shouted in bird-language. For when Mrs Pepperpot was small she could talk with animals and birds.

A big crow cawed: "Are you going to the moon with that balloon?"

"Not quite, I hope!" said Mrs Pepperpot, and she told them the whole story.

The birds all squawked with glee when they heard about
the corn and the bird-house she had got for them.

"But first you must help *me*," said Mrs Pepperpot. "I want you all
to hang on to this balloon string and guide me back to land on my
own doorstep."

So the birds clung to the string with their beaks and claws and, as
they flew down to Mrs Pepperpot's house, the balloon looked like a
kite with fancy bows tied to its tail.

When Mrs Pepperpot set foot on the ground she instantly grew to her normal size. So she waved goodbye to the birds and went indoors to wait for Mr Pepperpot.

It was late in the evening before Mr Pepperpot came home, tired and miserable after searching everywhere for his lost wife. He put his knapsack down in the hall and carried the sheaf of corn and the bird-house outside. But when he came in again he noticed that the mistletoe had disappeared.

"Oh well," he said sadly, "what does it matter now that Mrs Pepperpot is gone?"

He opened the door into the kitchen; there was the mistletoe hanging over the doorway and, under it, as large as life, stood Mrs Pepperpot!

"Darling husband!" she said, as she put her arms round his neck and gave him a great big smacking kiss. "Happy Christmas!"

Angela McAllister

THE SNOW ANGEL

Illustrated by Claire Fletcher

IT WAS THE FIRST SNOW MORNING. Elsa made giant's footsteps to
the frozen dewpond. She built snow castles, and she slid down the
slippery slope.

Then she found a secret place. Elsa lay on the snow blanket and
spread her arms like wings. She made the shape of an angel.

Elsa showed her friend Jack. "This is where a snow angel lay," she whispered. That Jack always thought her tales were true.

"I wish I could see a snow angel," he sighed, "more than anything in the whole wide world."

The next morning Jack found Elsa. He was very excited.

"I saw her! I saw the snow angel last night, sweeping away the snowdrifts. And she gave me a wish and I rode the big rabbit. And it's true, I really did." But Elsa just smiled. That Jack was always dreaming.

The next morning Jack looked everywhere for Elsa.

"The snow angel came again!" he said. "She melted the ice with her breath. And she gave me a wish, and all the fish were flying fish, even that old whiskery. And I saw it, I really saw it." But Elsa just smiled. That Jack was always telling stories.

The next morning Jack was waiting for Elsa.

"The swinging tree was so heavy with snow it was going to crash through the window, and the snow angel blew it all away. And she gave me a wish and all the icicles were made of sugar. And I ate one hundred and I really, really did." But Elsa just smiled. That Jack was a good pretender.

That night a fresh snow fall covered the giant's footsteps and the castles and the slippery slope. Everything was buried deep. But, when Elsa returned to the secret place, an angel's shape still glistened in the snow. Were those the wings she had made?

Gently Elsa lay down. She thought about Jack. She shut her eyes and made a wish. And when she sat up the snow wings began to grow.

First little snow buds, then long soft, white feathers unfolded and lifted her high amongst the trees!

Up and up and Elsa flew through the frosty air. She shook the branches, she stood on the treetops, she skimmed the stepping stream. Then low among the trees someone was hiding.

And Elsa flew.

All morning she flew with the snow angel in and out of the blue shadows, until the sun began to melt her wings.

One last swoop over the church spire then softly Elsa fell to earth.

Jack met Elsa at the slippery slope. He was very excited. "I didn't see a snow angel this morning . . . I saw two!"

Elsa looked up through the snowflakes and laughed. Maybe that Jack knew a true thing after all. "Come on then, Jack," she said, "let's make giant's footsteps in this snow."

Virginia Mayo

DON'T FORGET ME, FATHER CHRISTMAS

IT WAS CHRISTMAS EVE. Through the night, the snow had gently
fallen until it covered sleeping towns and villages where children
lay good in their beds, waiting for Father Christmas. Close to
midnight, most children were asleep, except for one: a baby who
was wide awake and gazing thoughtfully up at the sky.

Meanwhile, in his sleigh, Father Christmas was tired. He'd been to
every country with his great big sack - landed on rooftops, squeezed
through chimney-pots, and struggled up and down chimneys until
he had finally arrived at the last house.

Lizzie and Robert were fast asleep and never heard Father Christmas as he tiptoed up to the beds as carefully as he could with his bent back and aching feet. As he stuffed their stockings with toys, he was already thinking of that lovely cup of tea waiting for him back at the North Pole when he was finished.

He didn't notice a pair of eyes watching his every move from a dark corner across the room. Neither did he spot another red Christmas stocking dangling over the side of the cot.

The baby clapped his hands together.
Oh at last . . . there he is! OI! Me next, Father Christmas!
But Father Christmas was off out the door and back on to the roof.

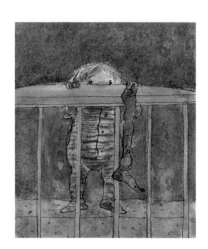

Just a minute . . . where are you going?

The baby was left quite alone. So he waited . . . and he waited.

It's all right. I'm sure he'll be back in a minute . . . He is COMING, isn't he? No! He can't . . . he can't have FORGOTTEN me! He HAS! He's forgotten me! I'm all alone, waiting with my stocking . . . and he's never going to come . . .

At first, the baby began to cry, then he sat up with a start, threw

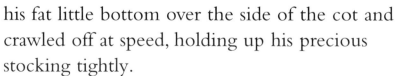

his fat little bottom over the side of the cot and crawled off at speed, holding up his precious stocking tightly.

Well, I'm not giving up just like that!

Up on the roof, the reindeer were surprised by the sight of a sooty baby's head appearing out of the chimney. "Good heavens!" cried a deer. "Did you see that?"

"Yes, I did," replied another. "Do you think he knows there's a baby on the roof ?"

Sadly, Father Christmas had his back to it all and had no idea that the furious baby was crying and pleading and shaking his fist at him.

119

"Reindeer away!" ordered Father
Christmas, climbing aboard the sleigh.
But the baby was not going to be stopped.
Wait for me . . . !

He grabbed hold of the sleigh as it began to rise slowly in the air.
Up and up he went, rising higher in the sky, holding tightly and never
daring to look down far below as houses, cities, fields and oceans
whizzed by. It was a good thing no one on the ground was watching.

121

Soon a small landing strip of lighted flares came into view in the middle of the snowy mountains of the North Pole. A crowd of elves had lined up outside Father Christmas's house to welcome him with a hot steaming cup of tea. As the reindeer were led away for a well-earned rest, one of the elves let out a cry: "Look at this!"

Everyone came running to see. "It's a baby!"

"Oh, Father Christmas, really! How could you? Didn't you know he was there?"

"But . . . but . . . how . . . ?" Father Christmas felt so silly he didn't know what to say. Then he saw the baby's stocking empty.

You FORGOT me!

The baby burst into tears.

"Right," said Father Christmas. "I know what we can do about that!'

So saying, he picked up the baby, dried his eyes and carried him to the workshop where the rest of the elves were packing and finishing off the last of the toys to be put away for next year.

By the time they reached the workshop, the news had reached the elves that silly old Father Christmas had brought a stowaway baby back on the sleigh.

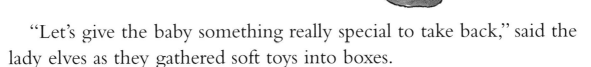

"Let's give the baby something really special to take back," said the lady elves as they gathered soft toys into boxes.

The baby was thrilled when he saw the workshop. Every toy he could want was there, but the biggest and best of them was a large brown bear and that was what the baby chose.

Father Christmas put on his leather jacket and gave the baby his red hat and coat to wear to keep him warm on his journey home.

123

By the time they got back to the baby's bedroom he was asleep and Father Christmas gently laid him in his cot without waking him, and slipped quietly away.

At first light of Christmas morning, Lizzie and Robert were up and rummaging through their Christmas stockings, eating their sweets and throwing off wrapping paper. The baby was usually the first one to wake up and yet there he was, flat out in his cot and not a sound.

"Do you think he's all right?" asked Lizzie.

"He's lying very still," said Robert, "pull his covers off !"

"Wake up, sleepy, it's Christmas Day!"

But the baby was awake. Up he sat with a wink . . . and a big red fluffy thing on top of his head.

"What on earth is he wearing?" cried the children.

Father Christmas had forgotten his hat!

John Bush
EMILINA HEDGEHOG
Illustrated by Peter Weevers

IN her cosy little room, snuggled up in bed,
Emilina Hedgehog pulls the covers to her head.
Peeking out by candlelight, she reads her favourite
  story,
Of how her great-grandfather won fortune, fame
  and glory.

Wilberforce was his name; a sailor bold was he,
Who discovered hedgehog continents across the
  Woodland Sea.
And there's a part that always brings a tear to
  Emmie's eyes,
When Wilberforce is knighted and the queen says,
  "Sir, arise."

But proud of her great-grandfather as Emilina is,
She's rather glad that *her* life is more quiet and safe
  than his.
There's no place that she'd rather be, of that she is
  quite sure,
Than snuggled in her winter bed - cosy and secure.

ACKNOWLEDGEMENTS

THE PUBLISHERS GRATEFULLY ACKNOWLEDGE THE FOLLOWING
AUTHORS AND ILLUSTRATORS:

'Wild Weather' from *Stories by Firelight* published by The Bodley Head,
© Shirley Hughes 1993

The Three Bears' Christmas Party published by Julia MacRae Books,
© text Maggie Russell 1992 © illustrations Anthony Lewis 1992

Simon and the Snow published by Hutchinson Children's Books,
© Bohem Press 1986

Penguin published by Hutchinson Children's Books,
© Susie Jenkin-Pearce 1988

Bad Mood Bear and the Big Present published by Hutchinson Children's Books,
© John Richardson 1993

Tiny Ted's Winter published by Hutchinson Children's Books,
© Peter Bowman 1994

Jolly Snow published by Hutchinson Children's Books,
© Jane Hissey 1991

'If Mooses Were Gooses' and 'Emilina Hedgehog' from *The Christmas Fox and Other Winter Poems*
published by Hutchinson Children's Books,
© text John Bush 1988 © illustrations Peter Weevers 1988

Frog in Winter published in a fully illustrated edition by Andersen Press,
© Max Velthuijs 1992

The Silver Christmas Tree published by The Bodley Head,
© Pat Hutchins 1974

The Mole Family's Christmas published by Jonathan Cape,
© text Russell Hoban 1969 © illustrations Lillian Hoban 1969

Mrs Pepperpot's Christmas published by Hutchinson Children's Books,
© text Alf Prøysen 1970 © illustrations Björn Berg 1970

The Snow Angel published by The Bodley Head,
© text Angela McAllister 1993 © illustrations Claire Fletcher 1993

Don't Forget Me, Father Christmas published by Hutchinson Children's Books,
© text Virginia Mayo 1999 © illustrations Virginia Mayo 1992